copyright

I0625631

# Disclaimer

This is a work of fiction. Names, characters, organizations, spots, occasions and occurrences are either the results of the creator's creative energy or utilized as a part of an invented way. Any similarity to real people, living or dead, or genuine occasions is absolutely adventitious.

ISBN:
eBook: 978-1-946792-00-6
print: 978-1-946792-01-3
audio/d :978-1-946792-02-0

© 2017 Urquhart Randolph

Published by Glofton llc

All rights held. No some portion of this production might be replicated, dispersed, or transmitted in any shape or by any methods, including photocopying, recording, or other electronic or mechanical strategies, without the earlier composed authorization of the distributer, aside from on account of brief citations encapsulated in basic audits and certain other noncommercial uses allowed by copyright law.

copyright

# Table of Contents

**VISIT US**
WWW.GLOFTON.COM
Enroll in our VIP list.
Be the first to be notified on our latest published book.
Downloading for free gifts.

copyright

# Unveiling a Dream

# Chapter One

"Another Saturday night, another gig... Life doesn't get any better than this."

Bill Masters' words brought a smile to Tim and Clark's faces. "Uncover", their band, seemed to be doing well. About a year ago, they signed a contract with "Merlin's", a fancy nightclub in Soho and, almost every time they performed, it was packed. Still, Roy Gabriel, lead guitarist and singer of the band didn't share their enthusiasm.

"I think it does." He spoke his mind, his face stiff, his deep, manly voice effective wiping the smile off Bill's face. "Look around you, boys. We're in a nightclub; not in Madison Square Garden."

"It's a start, Roy." Bill said. "I don't know about you, but I like the attention."

"We *all* like the attention." Roy raised his tone. "But, when are we going to...?"

"We're a *cover* band, man." Bill interrupted. "I get it; you want better things for yourself. We all do. But, let's face it: Without an album, it's never going to happen."

copyright

"That's why I've been posting videos of our gigs on YouTube." Tim interjected. "They don't have many views, though."

"Patience, big Roy." Bill patted him on the back. "Five hundred people have come to hear us. We can't let them down."

"Why would we do that to them?" Roy squinted at him.

"You look pretty upset, that's all." Bill remarked. "Trust me, brother. Good things will come."

"Let's hope they do." Roy sighed. At that moment, the music in the bar stopped altogether. A few whistles and cheers filled the air, as the lights were dimmed. Roy sucked in a deep breath, before passing by his fellow musicians and opened the door of the small dressing room, with the words of his good friend still ringing in his ears.

"Damn it. I hate to admit it, but Bill's got a point." He thought to himself, walking down the narrow corridor that led to the stage. "The **only way** to get out of this is making an album. But, I can't think about this anymore. I need to focus."

copyright

Roy could barely make out his black, electric guitar in the stand in front of him. After strapping it around his neck though, every negative thought fled his mind. Performing live was his childhood dream and it was at that moment that he realized that the number of people attending the venue did not really matter.

It would not change the sensation of the fine wood on his fingertips, nor would it affect his heartbeat. As every self-respecting musician, Roy had stage fright. He could feel sweat dripping down his braw; his thumb and index fingers were shaking, as he took a brown pick between them. Bill's keyboard introduction sent the crowd into a frenzy and for good reason: "Uncover" were going to play Cutting Crew's famous ballad "(I Just) Died In Your Arms Tonight". Seconds into the song, the club was filled with loud cheers.

The warm reception filled Roy's heart with confidence. Tightening his grip on his pick, he decided to give the crowd what they had been waiting for: A unique, majestic performance. He would have to cope with the sea of emotion that flooded his heart; Cutting Crew's ballad was the song that Emma Stinson, his high school sweetheart had once dedicated to him. However, he did not mind.

copyright

On the contrary, the memories he shared with her actually *helped* him. A massive spotlight was pointed on him, just before he closed his eyes. His voice was full of passion and conviction, as emotion poured out of him...

Every hair on his body was raised, as he sang the famous, international ballad. He would not open his eyes; for those few minutes, Roy was in his own world, a world that he and Emma had once created, full of fragrances, familiar faces, endless nights, full of talking, sex and laughing.

Every lyric brought back different memories, her reactions, their -numerous- fights and the times they made up, up until the point that she left him. Instinctively, he blocked that memory out.

Even after all this time, recollecting that moment hurt him deeply.

Roy had practiced that song on his guitar so many times that he could play it with his eyes closed. And, as its end got nearer, he understood that he would never get bored it, the same way that he would never get tired of remembering his good times with Emma.

copyright

Clark's final drum loop and Roy's downward strum concluded the song. The crowd burst into a loud round of applause, making his heart leap with joy. By now, stage fright was gone. Looking into them, he savored the moment, smiling to himself.

"Good evening, boys and girls." He spoke through his microphone. "How are you all doing?" The crowd responded with more cheers and whistles, turning his smile into a grin. "That's what I'm talking about. Now, let's get…" He paused, waiting for them to finish his sentence. "Rocked!" They cried, giving him the signal he had been waiting for. Roy's band began playing Def Leppard's "Let's Get Rocked". This time, they were even louder, as they rhythmically clapped their hands.

The night went on, with more and more, older and newer songs. Roy turned the stage into his personal playground, jamming with Tim or Bill and sometimes with Clark. Determined to enjoy this as much as he possibly could, he continued playing and singing for almost two hours non-stop.

Roy was having so much fun that they didn't even take a break that night.

copyright

Finally, twenty-eight songs later, the band held each other's hands and bowed down together to their audience. Roy was about to go back to the backstage area, when he sensed a firm grip on his shoulder. It was Joe Merlin, the elderly club owner.

"Wonderful performance tonight." He yelled in his ear, as the crowd roared into applause. "A record company rep is waiting for you in your dressing room."

"What?" Roy's voice became high-pitched, as he turned to Joe. "What's his name? Why didn't you say anything before?"

"I didn't want to stress you guys out." Joe explained. "It's not a 'he'. She says she wants to see you. Alone."

"Are you sure she's not a groupie?" Roy wondered.

"I know a groupie when I see one." Joe rejected that notion. "She is *not*. Go see her."

copyright

# Chapter Two

As one would expect, Joe's statement had triggered Roy's imagination. Excited by the fact that he would meet a record company representative, he couldn't wait to return to his dressing room.

Upon opening the door however, his jaw dropped to the floor. The woman waiting for him was none other than Emma Stinson. She looked even better than the 18-year old girl he remembered. 5'7", with long, light-brown, curly hair, curvaceous and with a bright smile on her beautiful face.

"Roy Gabriel." She spoke in her calm, feminine voice, rising from her seat. "God, it's been so long."

"Emma?" He whispered. "You're the rep?"

"That's right." She said with a nod, slowly walking up to him. "My boss told me about this new, promising band. He said 'They sound amazing.' You can't imagine my surprise, when I saw who their singer was."

"*Your* surprise?" Roy laughed. "I was expecting to find someone…"

"Old?" Emma inquired.

copyright

"Well, yeah." He admitted. "How have you been, Emma?"

"Very well, thank you." She attempted a business-like tone. "Now, about that band of yours. I represent 'Golden Media Records', you might have heard of…"

"Whoa, whoa, whoa." He interrupted, raising his hand to chest height, palm facing her. "We've not seen each other in more than ten years and you want to talk about *work*? What's the matter with you?"

"I don't have much time, Roy." Emma lowered her tone. "And, even if I did, a tiny dressing room is not the place to catch up, is it?"

"Maybe not." Roy reluctantly agreed. "How about a cup of coffee? How's tomorrow morning?"

Emma did not verbalize. Instead, she too lifted her left arm, her palm facing her. Roy was stunned to discover that she had a sparkling, engagement ring on. In a split second, any hope of reuniting with her was gone.

"Who's the lucky guy?" He murmured.

"My boss." She answered, dropping her arm. "Can we talk business now?"

"Go ahead." Roy urged, brushing past her.

copyright

"I only came here to let you know that we've been monitoring you and your band." Emma claimed. "I saw the last two songs you guys played. Ben is right; you guys do sound incredible. How long have you been playing together?"

"Six years, give or take." Roy said. "You weren't here from the beginning?"

"No, I was at a fundraiser." Emma replied. "Anyway, as much as I liked your show, I think I need to see a full concerto get clearer picture. When's your next gig?"

"Tomorrow night." He croaked.

"I'll see you tomorrow then." She said. "Goodnight."

Under any other circumstances, Roy would be ecstatic. Very soon, he would have a great chance to prove to a record company that his band was worth a lot more than just two shows a week in a nightclub. Nevertheless, Emma's attitude frustrated him so much that he would not even watch her leave. He grabbed a stool and sat down, leaning his back against the wall, as he shut his eyes.

His ex-girlfriend was nothing like he recalled. She was much friendlier and way more talkative than the stiff business executive who had just walked out the door.

copyright

"Smoking…" Bill's voice tore the silence. "The chick that just left. Smoking hot."

"That was Emma." Roy stated, staring down at the floor. "Or at least someone who looked a lot like her."

"Your girlfriend in high school?" All of a sudden, Bill's nasal voice became high-pitched. "The one who went off to college and broke your heart? *That* Emma?"

"Yep." Roy nodded, looking up at his friend. "Rich, stone cold and engaged to be married to some record company CEO."

"Oh, crap…" Bill sighed, running his hand through his hair. "What did you guys say?"

"Not much." Roy shrugged his shoulders. "Her fiancé likes us; so does she. She'll be here tomorrow night, too."

"That's great news!" Bill cheered. "I thought you'd be happy."

"I can't, Billy." Roy maintained. "The *one* girl I ever fell in love with is getting married. And she's different. She didn't even hug me, for old times' sake."

copyright

"Where the hell did my macho frontman go?" Bill teased him. "You never talk like that, Roy. Hey... You're not still in love with her, are you?"

"Is it that obvious?" Roy's voice was dripping with sarcasm.

"I hate to break it to you buddy, but you need to get over it." Bill suggested. "We've all been waiting for an opportunity like this. Go find someone else, have a good time, try to forget about this."

"A one-night-stand won't help." Roy disagreed. "Not this time."

"Just try to put this behind you, man." Bill continued. "It's going to be tough; I know. But to me, it looks like you don't have much choice. Now, let's go tell the others. We should be celebrating."

Roy spoke no further. Rising from his seat, he left the dressing room and soon joined his friends at the bar, still trying to wrap his head around his encounter with Emma. Tim and Clark were delighted to hear the news of signing a contract with a record company. Roy explained to them his situation, but it soon became clear to him that they were too happy to provide any advice or sympathy.

copyright

Deciding to follow Bill's advice, he went on to celebrate with them. Once again, a few fans showed their appreciation by chatting with them or asking for autographs.

"I'm done whining about you getting married to some rich prick, darling. Come tomorrow night, I'm going to show what you've been missing out on all these years. I don't know if playing our song is a good idea, but, if we do play it, it's going to be in the middle or at the end of our set list. Believe me, Emma. This concert will be much better and more emotional than you've ever imagined."

## Chapter Three

Roy went home in the early morning and, despite his exhaustion, he could not find peace. He barely slept; the set list kept swirling in his mind. It had to be entirely different.

His band would play some upbeat songs, but their gig on Sunday night would be dominated by ballads and love songs. They would have to include some stuff that they had never played before, but none of them would have a problem with that. They were all seasoned musicians.

Racking his brain, he came up with more than two dozen songs. Roy then called each and every one of them and arranged a quick rehearsal in the early afternoon. At first, his friends complained; they had hardly had enough rest, but he insisted, claiming that they had to do their absolute best that night. Each song was rehearsed at least twice and by the time they were finished, it was already 8:35pm.

They didn't even have time to go home and catch their breath; they went straight to "Merlin's", as their show was scheduled at 9:30.

The night before, Roy thought that he would be anxious; yet, this was not the case. He was oozing with confidence, but his friends were clearly nervous. Only minutes before they went on stage, he took a deep breath and addressed them:

"Alright kids." He started. "This is our night. We need to show that fact cat what we're made of. We're going to rock the shit out of this place and get what we deserve: A contract. Are you with me?"

"Yeah!" They all cried in one voice.

copyright

"Let's go!" Roy yelled, as the lights in the bar were dimmed. Even in the pale light, he was able to notice Emma, sat at a table nearest to the stage and to the left. Her fiancé looked exactly like the man he imagined:

Much older, somewhat overweight, with short, graying hair and a thick moustache. But this was not the time to comment on anybody's looks. His success depended on that very man's opinion; he had to give the performance of a lifetime.

Much to everybody's surprise, the first song they played that night was Eric Clapton's "Layla". Roy's passion poured out of him, as he started jamming the electric guitar introduction. He held his silver pick so tightly between his fingers that his fingertips quickly turned white. The roar of applause encouraged him; Emma's image would not even distract him. Driven by the desire to do much better for himself and his band, he looked into the crowd, as his friends joined him.

Indeed, their performance was much more powerful than any other night. Eric Clapton's rock anthem was not even over yet, when the crowd burst into a deafening, long round of applause. Ben and Emma clapped their hands, obviously excited by what they had just witnessed.

copyright

Roy stole a quick glance at her, but he would not stare, fearing that a possible misunderstanding could ruin everything.

Proceeding to the next phase of his plan, he passionately performed songs that he and Emma had danced to, when they were dating. In a matter of roughly two hours, Roy sang Pink Floyd, Bon Jovi, Deep Purple, Whitesnake and Guns 'n' Roses ballads. The crowd did not complain. If anything, they seemed to love every minute of it. As time went by, Emma stared more and spoke less to her fiancé.

Roy had most of her attention; she hardly threw a glance at the others. Even so however, he would not risk too much eye contact. Of course, he was intrigued. Part of him wanted to talk to her, ask her if she liked him or not, but he would not do such a thing. Instead, Roy preferred to keep singing and attempt to impress her and Ben even more if possible. All the same, the middle-aged executive did not stay there for long. Thirty or so minutes into the show, he wrote something on a piece of paper, handed it over to Emma and left.

copyright

It was a wonderful night. Energized by the crowd, "Uncover" played tirelessly for hours. None of them was willing to stop. Why would they? Their audience was in ecstasy and they would soon have what they had been after for years. Just after midnight, amid yet another roar of applause, Roy looked left, down at Emma.

"Thanks a lot for tonight, people." He spoke through his microphone, returning his gaze to the crowd. "You've been amazing tonight. I don't think I've ever had so much fun. Which is why I want to tell you a story: Regulars know that Cutting Crew's '(I Just) Died in Your Arms Tonight' is our opening song. But none of you knows why.

A long time ago, my girlfriend at the time dedicated it to me. I saw her again recently. It brought back memories, things I've been trying to forget. Anyway, this one's for her. One, two, three..."

Roy's words sent shockwaves down Emma's spine. She leaned her elbows on her table and put her head in her hands, as the sound of Bill's keyboard filled the air. Roy couldn't have wished for a better reaction. The cold woman he had encountered the previous night had disappeared. Emma was showing emotion and he was going to make sure that she didn't regret it.

copyright

Much to his disappointment though, his ex girlfriend was too overwhelmed to watch him sing. Seconds afterwards, she literally jumped from her seat and started pushing through the audience. For a moment, Roy was concerned that she would leave and not come back, but he quickly rejected that notion. After all, Emma was there for business.

The last round of applause was the longest and loudest of the night. Roy scanned the club, but she was nowhere to be seen. He checked the backstage area, but Emma was not there, either. One of the waiters informed him that he had noticed a brunette going out the back door. He was right; Roy found Emma in the dark, narrow alley behind the club, with her arms folded across her chest. The post lights on either side of the alley were dim, but their pale light revealed something that made his heart sink:

She had been crying. Tears were still rolling down her cheeks, as he laid his eyes upon her.

"What the hell did you *just* do?" Emma's voice was thick with emotion.

"The same thing I've been doing for almost a year now." He responded, his voice steady and calm. "There's nothing wrong with remembering the past."

copyright

"No. That's where you're *wrong*, Roy." She attempted an emphatic tone, leaning in towards him. "Let me jog your memory. Do you remember *why* we broke up?"

"Yeah." He confessed with a sigh. "You said I was 'emotionally unavailable.' That's just a fancy way of saying 'you wouldn't open up to me'."

"Exactly!" She exclaimed. "We went out for sixteen months and you wouldn't let me in. You kept saying 'I'm not a good talker. Whenever I need to say something, I just let my singing do the talking.' I liked it at first, but eventually, I got tired of it. Guess what, Roy. You can't always sing your way out of trouble."

"People change, Emma." He remarked. "You're right; I should have opened up to you. But, we were just kids back then. And God knows you're a lot different than the sweet girl I remember."

"I grew up." Emma stated, running her hand through her hair. "You've not changed. You still think that you're going to play the guitar and win me over, like you once did. I'm not eighteen anymore, Roy. This ship has sailed."

copyright

Roy was at a loss for words. Clearly, his plan had failed miserably. He couldn't force another word out of his throat. Emma pulled the small piece of paper that Ben had given her out of her pocket and handed it over to him, along with his business card.

"You are a very talented young man. Tomorrow morning, my office, 11:30. Don't be late.

Ben Richardson"

"Strictly business." She added, grabbing the door handle. "We'll be waiting for you."

## Chapter Four

With a heavy heart, Roy informed his friends about his appointment with Richardson. Predictably, they all had the same question: Why the record company representative didn't request to meet all of them. Roy could not provide an answer. Too saddened by Emma's rejection, he had forgotten to ask her. Whatever the reason, he would soon find out.

copyright

Something else bothered him, something that none of his fellow musicians would appreciate: The idea that he could soon answer to Emma's fiancé. If they were offered a contract, Ben would become his boss. More than that, he would often see them together and that would annoy him even more. Very soon, he was in a very difficult position and he had no idea what to do. At any rate, he owed it to himself to go to his appointment with Richardson.

"Golden Media Records" was the largest tenant of a massive, 42-story, steel tower on Fifth Avenue. Roy walked into the imposing building, unable to stop speculating on Ben's intentions.

The elevator stopped at the penthouse. Just like the rest of the tower, it was grey and cold, but rather quiet. Stepping off the empty car, Roy found himself in a large, wide corridor, with a single office in the upper right corner and an elderly woman sat at it, typing furiously.

"You must be Mr. Gabriel." She said, arising to her small stature. He nodded. "Follow me, please."

The door to Ben Richardson's office down the hall was open. He was standing behind a giant, glass façade, with a clear, unobstructed view of Manhattan, as she knocked on his door. He was much shorter than Roy, not more than 5'9".

copyright

"Thank you, Polly." He said, turning to them. "Leave us, please. Mr. Gabriel, how nice to finally meet you." He continued, offering his hand for a handshake.

"Hey." Roy croaked, shaking his hand. "You have a great view from up here."

"It is quite something, isn't it?" Ben smiled. "Have a seat."

Roy obliged, sitting at the black, leather couch to the right.

"You were fantastic last night." Ben couldn't hide his admiration. "You reminded me the music I used to listen to in my youth. Today's music is not so good."

"You're right about that." Roy agreed. "But today's music industry is not *just* about music. It's also about looks."

"Well said." Ben nodded. "Mr. Gabriel, I've been hearing lots of nice comments about you and your band. People seem to love you, but they all have one, big question: Why won't you play your own songs? Why do you just do covers?"

"It's what we're good at." Roy attempted a firm tone. "We've written a few songs, but we haven't recorded anything yet. Production is just too expensive."

copyright

"Tell me about it." Ben laughed. "What do you mean by 'we'?"

"I've written lyrics and music for most of them." Roy maintained. "Bill, our keyboardist has written music for two songs."

"I need to take a look at those." Ben said. "I'm going to be honest with you, Mr. Gabriel. We're only interested in you. We don't need the rest of your band."

"What?" Roy squeaked, unable to believe his ears. "*Just* me?" He pointed to himself.

"That's right." Ben affirmed. "You're a very talented young man, Roy. You have a gift. Now, like I said, I need to go over those songs of yours, but, even if I don't like them, there's no reason why you shouldn't sign a contract with us. We have dozens of songs available; we just don't have anyone with a good enough voice to sing them."

"I'm not doing this without my band!" Roy yelled, his stentorian voice echoing in the spacious office.

"You still haven't heard my offer." Ben smirked. "Two-year contract. Two hundred thousand. Think about it. FYI, I know about you and Emma. She didn't tell me anything, but it doesn't take Einstein to figure out that you two have history."

copyright

"How do you know?" Roy wondered.

"She got upset when I asked her to attend one of your venues. She started trying to find excuses not to go. Lame excuses, that is." Ben spoke in a steady tone. "I'm fifty two years old, Mr. Gabriel. I can understand when someone is lying to me. Now, take some to think about my offer. You don't have to answer right away. But, make sure to email me that material."

"I don't need any time." Roy's voice rumbled like thunder. "The answer is 'no'."

"Three hundred thousand." Ben's smile was wiped off his face. He even stared at Roy and would not even blink. "I'm going to make you rich, you stupid son of a bitch. *Fuck* your band. I'm going to make you so much money you can swim in it."

Roy struggled to keep his cool. He clenched his fists, shutting his eye, feeling his blood boiling in his veins. Whatever numbers Richardson had said did not matter. He had insulted one of the few things in life that he held dear: His band. The middle-aged executive had suggested him to leave them behind, betray their trust and effectively ruin something that had taken years to build.

copyright

"I'm going to pretend I didn't hear that." He grumbled, arising to his 6'3", impressive stature. "So long."

"What's the matter?" Ben's smirk reappeared. "What did I say?"

"Shut the fuck up, asshole!" Roy cried, his chest pumping up and down. "Or I swear to God, I'm going to beat the living shit out of you!"

Without much thought, he stormed out of Richardson's office, wishing that he'd never gone there. Emma's fiancé was clearly an unscrupulous man, who didn't care about anything else other than making money. Making his way out of the tower, Roy realized that he was burdened with the grim task of having to tell his friends about the outcome of his appointment. At the same time, though, he was relieved that Richardson was definitely *not* going to become his boss.

"I'm really sorry, you guys." He thought to himself. "At least we won't have to answer to that prick. You could have done a lot better, Emma. He's old enough to be your father, but that's not really the problem. His greed makes me sick…"

copyright

# Chapter Five

The events of the past few days had taken a huge toll on Roy. He had barely slept or eaten and felt emotionally drained. Emma's rejection had affected him and Richardson's proposal was sure to devastate the band. He was not ready to face them just yet; the only thing on his mind was getting a good rest.

So, he returned to his third-story apartment on 143rd Street and hurriedly lay in bed.

In spite of his fatigue, Roy could not relax at all. He couldn't help but imagine the faces of his friends, as he told them about his appointment with Richardson.

"I'm more than sure they're going to tell me to sign the damn contract. They love me; they want what's best for me. But I love them, too. I can't just leave them hanging. Damn you, Richardson…"

The irritating sound of his apartment buzzer interrupted his thoughts and shattered any hope he had of getting some **much-needed** rest. He lazily got up and went to his front door.

"Who is it?"

"Hey, Roy." His ears were filled with a familiar, female voice. It was Emma.

copyright

"Come on up." He said, trying to overcome his initial surprise. He wasn't expecting to see her, especially after what she had said to him the night before. Upon answering his door, he realized that there was something different about her. She no longer resembled the angry, frustrated woman who had reprimanded him in the alley. Instead, she looked calm; sad even.

"I think I owe you an apology." Her tone was much lower.

"Come in." He urged. "What are you doing here, Emma? You were more than clear last night."

"I was." She admitted, passing him by. "I was a little too hard on you. I mean, we hadn't seen each other in a long time and I acted like I was…" She faltered. "Mad at you or something."

"Water under the bridge. Sit." He muttered, pointing at the kitchen table to the left.

"Ben told me about this morning." Emma sighed. "You turned down $300,000? I'm impressed."

"Well, you shouldn't." Roy shook his head sideways. "I would never turn my back on those three."

copyright

"You made the right call." She commented. "Not just because you would betray your buddies."

"Why do you say that?" He was intrigued.

"If you read the contract, you'd realize that you wouldn't just have to do a couple of albums. The company would pretty much own you. You'd have to travel across the States anytime they wanted, sing at fundraisers, galas and do exactly what they said. In other words, you'd become..."

"Their bitch." He finished her sentence.

"Yeah." She said with a nod. "Something like that. I'm sorry, Roy. You must be devastated."

"Honestly?" Roy snorted. "What you've told me over the past few days hurt a lot more than what that asshole suggested."

"I was a little too blunt." She confessed, as a smile of embarrassment spread across her face. "That's why I owed you an apology. By the way, I've never seen such a contract in my whole life. I've been working there for nearly two years and our artists are treated a lot more fairly."

"Maybe because none of them used to go out with you." He winked at her.

copyright

"He…"

"He knows about us." Roy informed. "He told me. Richardson thought he could buy me out. I'm not for sale."

"Son of a bitch…" Emma whispered. "No wonder he's being acting weird these days."

"What the hell did you see in him?" He asked, a hint of sarcasm in his voice. "He's almost twice our age, he's fat and not really…"

"Let's talk about something else." She interjected. "Please."

Roy's initial thought was to insist. It was obvious to him that discussing her relationship with Ben was not exactly her favorite topic. Nevertheless, he would not force the issue.

"Ok." He shrugged. "You said you wanted to apologize to me. The way I see it, there's only one way for you to do that."

"What's that?"

"*One* date." He raised his index in the air. "That's all I'm asking."

"Oh, God…" Emma let out an exasperated gasp. "Why are you doing this?"

"Because I want to see the fun, relaxed girl I used to date, one last time." He explained. "Not the tight-ass business executive."

"I'm right here!" Emma opened her eyes wide.

"Yeah, talking about business." He complained. "I just need a few hours of your precious time. I won't bother you again. I promise."

"Ok." The single word that came out of her mouth filled his heart with joy. "But we can't be seen together in public. Where are we going to go?"

"Bill's sister owns a bar in Brooklyn It's pretty secluded. I'll text you the address." He spoke in a gentle voice, looking deep into her big, hazel eyes. "When are you available?"

"Ben's out of town tonight." She said. "Meet you there? Say, 9pm?"

"Alright." A blissful smile formed on his face.

"It's a date then, Emma. God, I've missed going out with you. We always had so much fun together. Teasing each other, laughing, dancing…

copyright

One last time, baby. And, if I can't convince you to stay with me, so be it. Go on, marry him. Trust me, though. After tonight, that old fart will be nothing more than a bad memory…"

# Chapter Six

Eagerly anticipating to see Emma again, Roy arrived at "Ginger's" bar thirty minutes early. It was small, but tastefully decorated, with posters of rock stars lining its walls and numerous, red, green and blue spotlights on the ceiling. Sadly, he had to do what he had been avoiding since that morning: Tell his friends about the outcome of his appointment with Richardson, as he found them all at the bar, having drinks, chuckling and being loud as usual.

"Hey!" Bill cheered, hopping off his stool. "A big round of applause for our lead singer and guitar player extraordinaire, Mr. Roy Gabriel!"

Roy's face remained stiff, as he approached them. He wouldn't speak, hoping that his prolonged silence and his expression would render talking unnecessary. To no avail. Bill, Tim and Clark would not stop cheering and celebrating. As a matter of fact, Roy had to bang his hand against his counter to draw their attention.

copyright

"I have some bad news, boys." He spoke, sucking in a deep breath. "The record company wanted me. Just me, not you."

The news hit them like a wrecking ball. In a split second, they all went silent. Bill grabbed his stool and threw it against the wall across from him, turning quite a few heads on the other side of the bar, whereas Tim tossed his glass down on the marble floor. On the other hand, Clark preferred to run his hands through his long, blond hair, mumbling gibberish.

"This is bullshit!" Bill cried, his nasal voice audible over the soft music playing from the speakers. "What did you tell them?"

"What do you think?" Roy tried to keep his cool. "I wasn't going to betray you, guys. Not today, not ever. You'd hate my guts if I signed that contract, not to mention I'd become their property."

His last statement put a faint smile on their faces. Tim and Clarke glanced at each other, right before Bill hugged him. Very soon, Roy was lost in a big, group hug. He was a little embarrassed, but he was not going to complain. This was their way of showing their appreciation and any words that came out of his mouth could ruin the moment.

"You're all heart, Roy." Bill murmured.

copyright

"Thanks a lot, Billy." Roy smiled, pulling out of their embrace. "Let me remind you what you said the other night. Good things will come."

"You bet your ass they will." Bill returned the smile. "Anyway, what's up? We weren't expecting you."

"I have a date with Emma." Roy grinned. He had barely finished his sentence, when Emma walked into the bar, the click-clacking of her heels getting his attention. And, before either of them could say a word, the sound of Eric Clapton's "Wonderful Tonight" gave Roy an idea. He grabbed her by the wrist and led her to the dance floor down the hall. Emma could hardly keep up, but he would not stop.

As they reached it, he turned around to face her. He placed his hand on her left hip side and grabbed her right hand. Roy then held it up at shoulder level, so that their arms were bent upward from the elbow. Emma put her left hand on his right shoulder, bending her head slightly towards him.

"I'm sorry." He said in a soft voice. "I just really love that song."

"It's ok." She assured. "I'd forgotten how…"

copyright

"Shhhhh…" He brought his index finger to his lips, looking down into her eyes. "Now is not the time for words."

Getting lost in the warm look in her eyes, he pulled her closer. There was no tension on her face; indeed, Emma resembled more of the girl he had once fallen in love with. He leaned in towards her and whispered in her ear:

"I've missed dancing with you."

She did not utter a word. A hesitant smile spread across her glorious face, as the magic of Eric Clapton's ballad flooded their hearts with emotion…

Even more memories rushed through his mind, as they danced again for the first time in more than a decade. Roy had been lucky; they had danced to that song many times in the past. Romantic and beautiful, it sent shivers down his spine. Happily, Eric Clapton was one of her favorite artists. Emma used to talk about his albums for hours, even though most her friends used to taunt her about her obsession with an old rock legend such as him. However, she never paid any attention to their nasty comments and neither did he. Roy and Emma like almost exactly the same music. It was one of the many things that had brought them together in the first place.

copyright

Second by second, her face loosened even further. Roy was blissful; he had missed her relaxed expression so much that he often caught himself remembering the times when he had seen her sunbathing or just sleeping.

This was the main reason why her attitude the previous night had shocked him so deeply. Much to his liking though, that stiff, bossy woman had vanished. In her stead was the girl that he vividly remembered and cherished. And nothing could make him happier than that.

The romantic ballad was slowly fading out, as Roy slid his hand up her back. He leaned forward, until her ample lips were just inches from his face. As much as he would love to kiss her, he had to resist the temptation. Their date was only just getting started; anything impulsive could destroy everything. Therefore, he chose to give her a sweet smile, take her by the hand and lead her to the nearest table.

"Always unpredictable." She remarked, taking a seat.

"There's nothing wrong with being spontaneous." He claimed. "You used to love that."

"You said you'd changed." Emma said. "I don't see any changes."

copyright

"Well…" Roy heaved a long, heavy sigh. "When you and I broke up, I made a promise to myself: Share more, be more forward. To be honest, I regretted it. Not all women like openness in men."

"Actually, most of them do." She pointed out. "They appreciate it when their boyfriend confides in them."

"What happened to you, darling?" He smirked, unable to shake the feeling that the reason why she was marrying a man like Richardson was pure greed. "I thought you'd never marry someone for money."

"You think I'm marrying Ben for money?" Emma's sweet voice turned into a high-pitched squeal.

"Are you saying you're not?" Roy insisted. "Come on, Emma. That guy could be your father, for crying out loud."

He regretted to ever make that kind of suggestion, but he had been meaning to ask her that question since the moment he saw her fiancé. Roy expected her to snap at him; yet, she did no such thing. Instead, Emma lay back in her seat and dropped her gaze from him, crossing her arms over her chest.

"I'm sorry." He spoke in a mellow tone. "I shouldn't have said that."

copyright

"It's a sham." She said, as her eyes shot up to meet his gaze. "This engagement is a sham. About two years ago, my folks were neck-deep in debt. They were about to get evicted, they hadn't paid their mortgage in months. I was unemployed. I saw an ad online. Ben needed a new PA; at least, that's what the ad said. I called them, we arranged an interview. They said they'd call me in due time. But, I couldn't afford to wait; I needed the money. I practically begged them to hire me, said I'd do anything to get that job." Emma spoke in sighs. Roy bit his lower lip, in an obvious attempt to keep his mouth shut.

Her revelation had stunned him; still, she had lied to him from the beginning and he was struggling to keep his cool. The idea of storming out of the bar ran through his mind, but he was in such a state of shock that he could not even move.

"Then, Ben told me what the ad was *really* about." Emma went on. "He'd recently discovered that his father had included a special term in his will, according to which he'd have to be married or engaged to be married, in order to inherit his father's fortune.

The old man had cancer; the doctors had given him five to six months. He's tough, though.

copyright

He's still alive. Ben asked if I could pretend to be his fiancé, until his father died. In return, I wouldn't be just his PA, but a well-paid executive. He'd also give me the money to pay off my folks' debt. I said 'yes' right away."

"Dear God..." A whisper of despair left his lips, as she finished her narrative. "So... This was all an act?"

"I'm afraid so." She affirmed. "I'm sorry I lied to you, but I had no choice."

"Why didn't he ask his ex to marry him again?" Roy posed a question. "He's been married before, hasn't he?"

"There's no ex, Roy. Ben is gay." Emma's short sentence deepened his shock. Suddenly, the air around him had become too thick. Her revelations had overwhelmed him; he needed some fresh air. Roy rose from his seat and headed towards the door, in the hope that the sensation of the cool breeze in his face would help him clear his thoughts. His friends tried to stop him, but he wouldn't even turn to them.

With the buzzing of the soft music still in his ears, he pushed the heavy door open. A strong gust of wind tugged at his short, brown hair, as he stepped outside. Luckily for him, the narrow road was empty and quiet. Within seconds though, he realized that he wasn't alone.

copyright

The cold sensation of steel on his right temple and the sound of a gun cocking sent adrenaline rushing through his veins.

"There's a word for people like you." He heard Ben's hoarse voice. "Sucker. That's what you are, kid. A big-time sucker. Where's that whore?"

"Ben!" Emma's voice reeked of fear, as she stopped behind Roy. "What are you doing?! Put the gun down! Please!"

Ben then attempted to turn his gun towards her. Roy had to act fast. He elbowed Ben hard in the stomach. A scream of pain escaped him, as his gun slipped through his fingers. Gritting his teeth, Roy turned towards him and grabbed him by the collar of his coat. A tremendous blow to his opponent's jaw sent him ten feet along the pavement.

Fuming with rage, Roy hurtled towards him and dropped to his knees beside him. Just when he was about to hit him again though, Emma's voice stopped him.

"Roy, please!" She cried. "Don't!"

"We had a deal, you bitch…" Ben groaned, as a drop of blood rolled down his chin. "Pictures of you two are all over the internet."

copyright

"There's nothing go on between us!" Emma maintained. "We're just two friends catching up."

"Tell that to the press." Ben said. "You're fired."

"No…" She whispered, a look of terror spreading across her face. "I've done nothing wrong here!"

"Bullshit!" Ben yelled. "You've fucked it all up!"

Roy had heard enough. Unwilling to control himself anymore, he punched Ben so hard in the face that his head was rocked back. But then, he turned his attention to Emma. Devastated as she was, she burst into loud tears. He bounced up, turned around to face her and took her in his embrace, at the same time feeling guilty over the fact that their date had cost her her job.

"I'm really sorry, Emma." He whispered, caressing her hair. "This is all my fault."

"No…" She sniffled. "It's not. Please, take me home."

copyright

# Chapter Seven

The long drive back to Manhattan would give a good chance to Roy to reflect on what had just transpired. After all, it was more than obvious that Emma was in no condition to speak. For the first fifteen minutes or so, she kept weeping.

"If I knew I was going to get you fired, I wouldn't have asked you out." He said to himself. "I feel terrible about this."

Roy was getting more guilt-ridden by the minute. He simply could not fathom the harm he had caused her. Once again, he had made her cry. He was dying to tell her how sorry he was, but he would not start a conversation.

"It's amazing how quickly people can turn against you." She concluded, turning her head to the left to face him. "I mean, just a week ago he said he was going to give me a raise."

"I don't know about that." Roy shrugged. "But I do know one thing: I've not missed seeing you cry."

"There's no need to feel guilty about this." Emma made her voice sound even sweeter. "The more I think about it, the more I think it was just a matter of time."

copyright

"That doesn't make me feel any better." He sighed. "Anyway, what's your address?"

"2246, 15th Street. But I don't want to be alone right now. Let's go to your place." Her suggestion brought a smile to his face. Indeed, Roy was delighted. In an instant, he imagined how they would spend their first night together in more than ten years.

"I'd really love to lay my hands on you, Emma. Just thinking about it drives me crazy. But I don't think I'd mind if we just spent the night talking. You're back. That's all that matters."

Roy and Emma confined their conversations to generalities for the remainder of the drive. As his apartment building got closer, she seemed to feel better and more relaxed, proving to him that she did not accuse him of anything. Emma's sweet, hearty laughter reminded him of much simpler times. Minute after minute, he sensed his heart beating faster and faster.

Unlocking his front door, he let her in. Closing it behind him, he was about to verbalize, but Emma did not allow him to. She put her hands on his broad chest and pushed him back, looking deep into his eyes.

copyright

"I really liked what you did for me tonight." She said, her voice husky, as she slid her hands up his body.

"I never stopped loving you, Emma." He confessed with a whisper, wrapping his arms around her back. Roy tilted his head down to meet her lips, as her tender hands reached his neck. Their mouths joined in a long, passionate kiss that sent his adrenaline into the ozone layer. Roy's heart was racing; at last, the only woman he had ever fallen in love with was back in his arms.

He peeled off her coat, as their kiss deepened. Then, Roy pulled her blouse up and over her head. Emma's intoxicating scent filled his nostrils, as he claimed her lips once more. She circled her arms around his neck, as he put his big, strong hands on her hips. Emma hooked her left leg around his hip. She had a grey, knee-long skirt on and black pantyhose.

He couldn't resist the temptation to feel the smooth nylons in his palms. So, Roy took his right hand off of her body and placed it below her knee.

"Touch me, baby…" She whispered in his mouth, as his hand slowly traveled up her leg. But, as he soon discovered, Emma was not wearing pantyhose.

copyright

Instead, she had stockings on. His manhood twitched, as his fingers made contact with the supple flesh of her thigh. A deep groan escaped him, just before he ran his other hand up her back. He grabbed her lace bra, but he needed his other hand to unhook it. But Emma seemed to enjoy his caress on her leg too much to allow him to remove his hand from her. She reached behind her back and unhooked her bra. It fell on the hardwood floor, as Roy stroked her upper back. Entwining his arm around her, he pulled her closer and spun her around. In a swift move, he pinned her against the door.

Emma tilted her head back, exposing her neck, as her breath got heavier. His hand crept around her back, as he trailed soft kisses across her jawline. The mere thought of touching her big breasts was enough to give him an instant erection. Roy's lips made their way down her neck, as she placed her hands on his shoulders.

With her short sighs filling his ears, he ran his right hand up her leg and her body. She put it back down on the floor, as he cupped her breasts.

Roy squeezed them first and then pressed them together, planting soft kisses all over her chest. He trapped her nipples between his fingers, as she slid her right hand across his shoulder. Pinching her right nipple lightly, he stuck his hot, wet tongue out.

copyright

"Oh, my God…" She whimpered, squeezing her eyes shut, as he ran his tongue over her erogenous zone, squeezing her breasts at the same time. Emma's hands slid up his neck, as he pulled her nipple into his mouth. A gentle bite forced a loud moan out of her, as she slipped her hands into his hair. Roy licked the sensitive area around her nipple, enjoying her featherlike touch, feeling his cock getting wetter by the second. As much as he liked the whole thing though, he knew that taking her to bed would be much, *much* better. Therefore, he ran both hands down her midsection and grabbed her by the hips.

Pushing her body upwards, he lifted her off her feet. Her playful gasp of surprise and her broad smile made his heart flutter. Roy turned his body left and started walking down the corridor that led to his bedroom, as she wrapped her arms around his neck.

Pulling him closer, Emma tilted her head down once again. Their fiery kiss sent him one stop closer to heaven.

Roy eased her down on his bed and began to get rid of his clothes, maintaining eye contact with her. Her husky smile beckoned him, as she unbuttoned her skirt.

copyright

She pulled it down, exposing her long, shapely legs. Within seconds, she rolled her gaze down his body, fixing it on his chiseled abs. Emma licked her upper lip like a hungry predator, as he scanned her body, from bottom to top.

"Hottest thing alive..." He muttered, just before he climbed into bed. Hooking his thumbs into the waistband of her black thong, he slowly pulled it down and off her feet. Eager to taste her, he planted long, sensual kisses along her stomach. The sweet scent of her pussy juices soon filled his nostrils, as he reached her bellybutton.

He would not waste any more time. Once more sticking his tongue out, he ran it down her body, as she slightly spread her legs. Roy stroked her inner thighs, as the tip of his tongue made contact with her hard, swollen clit.

"Yeah, baby..." She moaned, pressing her crotch against his mouth. The taste of her juices overwhelmed him, but something else added to his arousal even more: Emma was soaking wet. His lips closed around her erogenous zone, as he squeezed her thighs. Roy felt her hands on his head. She grabbed fistfuls of his hair, as he sucked her clit into his mouth.

copyright

Flicking his tongue across it, he caressed her legs, feeling her juices flowing down his tongue. Emma's moans were getting louder and louder. She pressed his head against her, as he nipped at her clit. Roy moved his right hand up and led it to her entrance.

He sensed moisture on the tip of his index finger. Without much thought, he pushed it into her, running his tongue down her pussy.

"That's it, baby!" Emma's loud groan encouraged him to continue. She threw her head back, biting her lower lip, loving the attention. Pushing his finger deep inside her, he laid long, hot kisses all over her pussy, tasting more and more of her juices. The pronounced flexing of her pussy muscles was a clear sign that her orgasm was very close indeed. Willing to offer her a powerful climax, Roy slipped his middle finger into her as well, as his tongue returned to her clit.

Licking it in circles, he fastened his pace. Emma was so wet that her juices were dripping down his slender fingers, as her body trembled violently, her sexy, loud moans filling his bedroom. The heat in her pussy increased, as she was overwhelmed by a long, shuddering orgasm that took her breath away. Roy slowly pulled his fingers out of her and led them to his mouth. He licked her juices off, before opening his eyes.

copyright

"God, you look so sexy, baby…" He spoke in his deep, manly voice, as she gasped for breath. Emma did not utter a word. She leaned forward and grabbed him by the wrists, with a big smile of contentment on her glorious face. Entwining her arms around his massive back, she held him close, bringing his mouth directly over hers. Once more, their lips locked in a hot, sensual kiss. Roy rubbed his 8-inch long, throbbing cock against her clit, teasing her, but he was so turned on that he could not keep this up for long. He guided it to her entrance, just before she entwined her legs around his hips.

"Fuck me…" She whispered in his mouth. "Fuck me hard."

Of course, Roy needed no encouragement and he was way too aroused to even consider a slow-paced session. Sliding his rock hard cock deep inside her, he put his right hand on her upper outer thigh, feeling his manhood getting drenched by her juices.

A gasp of arousal left her lips, as she felt his entire length in her depths. Emma dug her long fingernails into the firm flesh of his upper back. Taken over by lust, he started thrusting her dripping wet pussy, taken over by lust.

copyright

Their tongues danced against each other, as he pounded her, her muffled moans in his mouth sending him to heaven. Emma tilted her head back yet again, unable to keep up their kiss, writhing under him. Roy leaned back, desperate to catch a glimpse of her breasts. She raised her legs in the air, as he sat on his knees. Then, he put her legs over his shoulders and penetrated her again.

"God, you're so deep…" Emma whimpered, as his big, stiff cock filled her up. Tiny drops of sweat were rolling down his rock hard pecks. The feel of her nylons on his chest drove Roy crazy with lust. Fixing his gaze on her pussy, he began to thrust her, faster and harder than before. She grabbed the sheets, watching his abs flexing with every thrust, as he sent waves of pleasure coursing through her body.

Her large, juicy breasts were bouncing back and forth, his loud, aggressive moans audible over hers, his big, heavy balls slapping against her flesh. He was coaxing her relentlessly towards her second orgasm that night and, even though he knew that he would not be able to last much longer, he would not stop.

copyright

"I'm going to come, baby!" Her husky moan bounced off the walls of his bedroom and the corridor outside. Roy quickened his pace, rolling his gaze up her body. The sight of her bouncing breasts overwhelmed him. Her body started quivering, as an even more powerful orgasm literally ripped through her. Roy felt her ample juices flowing down his throbbing cock. He could not take it anymore.

Pulling out, he grabbed his cock and jerked it a few times, before spurting a huge load of semen all over her stomach. Panting for breath, he tumbled into bed beside her...

# Chapter Eight

Emma laid her head on his chest, purring like a contented cat. Roy circled his left arm around her neck and pulled her closer, burying his face into her hair.

"Somebody's learned new moves..." She teased him, kissing him on the chest.

"Well..." He snorted. "Somebody's finally mastered the art of seduction. I don't get it, though. What did I do that you liked so much?"

"You were there for me." Emma whispered, looking up at him. "You soothed me; you were my friend. Old Roy wouldn't do that."

copyright

"I told you." He smiled down at her. "I told you I was different."

"Actions speak louder than words, Roy." She put a little force in her voice. "I think I need to thank you."

"For what?" He got curious. "Getting you fired?"

"No." She chirped. "For setting me free. I couldn't wait to leave that job."

"You're kidding me, right?" Roy wondered. "I thought you liked it there."

"I liked the money." Emma confessed. "But, other than that, it's the most boring job I've ever had to do. It was like time stood still in that place. I kept wondering when his father would die and put me out of my misery."

"Then why did you cry when he fired you?" He interjected one more question, intensifying his stare.

"Because I was wrongfully accused." She explained. "I did everything in my power to avoid you. I wouldn't go out with you; I was even *rude* to you. What else could I have done?"

"Punch me?" He laughed.

copyright

"It did cross my mind." She teased him. "But, I couldn't do that. You've been really good to me these past few days."

"I still can't believe you're here, Emma." Roy confessed, his voice low as he caressed her hair. "I thought you'd never give me a chance."

"A *second* chance." Emma corrected him. "You deserve it. *We* deserve it. You may think you hurt me tonight, but I believe I hurt you by getting you in touch with that scumbag. I had no idea he'd treat you like that."

"Please don't make me repeat myself." He politely requested. "It's all over. I didn't lose my job. *You* did. What are you going to do now?"

"I don't know." She shrugged. "I haven't had the chance to think about it, but I'd like to help you promote your band."

"Really?" Roy was intrigued. "How?"

"I know quite a few people in the business. You guys are talented; I'm sure you'll be offered a contract." Emma attempted a confident tone. "But, I'll need you to promise me something."

"What?"

"That you won't change." She lowered her sweet voice. "I really like this new Roy. He's a lot more thoughtful; a lot more caring."

copyright

"Cross my heart." He whispered. Emma snuggled up against him, as a sweet smile formed on her face. Roy caressed her wrist, as she brought her mouth directly over his. Her tender kiss made his heart flutter for the second time that night. Losing himself in the moment, he ran his hands up her back, caressing her smooth skin.

For many years, Roy Gabriel had been trying to find someone that resembled Emma. Whenever he believed that a woman was worth his attention, he would open up to her, often with catastrophic consequences. Most women hurt him, but he didn't give up. In a twist of fate, he ran into her. Her engagement to a rich executive saddened him, but did not deter him. Emma's fiancé tried to lure him with a huge contract. Nevertheless, Roy was a man of honor.

He would not betray his fellow musicians. The same man became responsible for shattering their dream. But Roy had another dream, one that no one, not even a man as powerful as Richardson could not destroy: Reconnecting with his high school sweetheart, Emma Stinson. Now that she was back in his life, he was determined to hold on to her, no matter the cost...

copyright

I write under the pseudonym: Urquhart Randolph. I like to write great romance stories that take you on a blazing journey - tears, laughter (may be both) or just a steamy hot fun (perhaps all of them).

Please... leave a review, regardless if you think my book deserves 1* or 5 * let me know if you had enjoyed this great story?

THANK YOU ☺

VISIT US
WWW.GLOFTON.COM
Enroll in our VIP list.
Be the first to be notified on our latest published book.
Downloading for free gifts.

www.ingramcontent.com/pod-product-compliance
Lightning Source LLC
Chambersburg PA
CBHW050912120626
46552CB00004B/1540